This book belongs to

Chirp!

Go to Bed CRICKET

Written by Lucas Wurtz Illustrated by Galina Moleskine

© Copyright 2021
Published by ShockOwl LLC, 2021
All Rights Reserved

Harvey, you better wash up and brush your teeth. Its time for bed sweetie.

"Mom can I finish my show? It's just about done. I'll go to bed soon I promise."

You can finish it, but you need to go to bed soon.

"You have a big day
at school tomorrow."

Thanks mom, I promise it wont be much longer!

XOXO
Ok! I love you Harvey, Goodnight.

Chirp! Chirp!
Chirp!

Chirp!
Chirp!
Chirp!

Go to bed Cricket!
You're being too loud!

Chirp!
Chirp!
Chirp!
Chirp!
Chirp!
Chirp!
Chirp!

Ugh!
Go to bed Cricket!

MILK

Chirp! Chirp!
Chirp!

Go to bed Cricket!

Chirp! Chirp!
Chirp!

Go to bed Cricket!

Zzz

Chirp!
Chirp!
Chirp!

CRICKET! PLEASE GO TO BED!!!

Goodnight Cricket.

Zzz

Chirp!